P9-BTY-919

The Night Before Christmas

Silverton School Library
1160 Snowden
Box 128
Silverton, CO 81433

The Night Before

POEM BY

CLEMENT MOORE

SCHOLASTIC INC.

New York Toronto London Auckland Sydney
Mexico City New Delhi Hong Kong

Book designed by Gunta Alexander. Text set in Zaph International.
Airbrush backgrounds by Joseph Hearne.

No part of this publication may be reproduced in whole or in part, or stored in a retrieval system, or
transmitted in any form or by any means, electronic, mechanical, photocopying, recording, or otherwise,
without written permission of the publisher. For information regarding permission, write to
Penguin Putnam Inc., 375 Hudson Street, New York, NY 10014

ISBN 0-590-68922-3

Illustrations copyright © by Jan Brett. All rights reserved.
Published by Scholastic Inc., 555 Broadway, New York, NY 10012,
by arrangement with Penguin Putnam Inc.
SCHOLASTIC and associated logos are trademarks and/or registered
trademarks of Scholastic Inc.

12 11 10 9 8 7 6 5 4 3 2 1   8 9/9 0 1 2 3/0

Printed in the U.S.A.   36

First Scholastic printing, November 1998

For Gregory, Sophie and Lee Tsairis

'**T**was the night before Christmas,
when all through the house
not a creature was stirring, not even a mouse.

The stockings were hung by the chimney with care,
in hopes that St. Nicholas soon would be there.
The children were nestled all snug in their beds,

while visions of sugar-plums danced in their heads.
And Mamma in her kerchief, and I in my cap,
had just settled down for a long winter's nap,

When out on the lawn there rose such a clatter,
I sprang from my bed to see what was the matter.
Away to the window I flew like a flash,
tore open the shutters and threw up the sash.
The moon on the breast of the new-fallen snow

gave a luster of mid-day to objects below,
when, what to my wondering eyes should appear,
but a miniature sleigh, and eight tiny reindeer,
with a little old driver, so lively and quick,
I knew in a moment it must be St. Nick.

More rapid than eagles his coursers they came,
and he whistled, and shouted, and called them by name,
"Now Dasher, now Dancer! Now, Prancer and Vixen!
On, Comet! On, Cupid! On, Donder and Blitzen!

To the top of the porch, to the top of the wall,
now, dash away, dash away, dash away all!"
As dry leaves that before the wild hurricane fly,
when they meet with an obstacle, mount to the sky,
so up to the house-top the coursers they flew,
with a sleigh full of toys—and St. Nicholas too.

RED LION INN

And then in a twinkling I heard on the roof
the prancing and pawing of each little hoof.
As I drew in my head, and was turning around,
down the chimney St. Nicholas came with a bound.

He was dressed all in fur, from his head to his foot,
and his clothes were all tarnished with ashes and soot.
A bundle of toys he had flung on his back,
and he looked like a peddler just opening his pack.

His eyes—how they twinkled! His dimples how merry!
His cheeks were like roses, his nose like a cherry!
His droll little mouth was drawn up like a bow,
and the beard on his chin was as white as the snow.

The stump of a pipe he held tight in his teeth,
and the smoke it encircled his head like a wreath.
He had a broad face and a little round belly,
that shook when he laughed like a bowlful of jelly.

He was chubby and plump, a right jolly old elf,
and I laughed when I saw him, in spite of myself.
A wink of his eye and a twist of his head,
soon gave me to know I had nothing to dread.

He spoke not a word, but went straight to his work,
and filled all the stockings, then turned with a jerk.

And laying his finger aside of his nose,
and giving a nod, up the chimney he rose.

He sprang to his sleigh,
to his team gave a whistle,

And away they all flew
like the down on a thistle.
But I heard him exclaim,
ere he drove out of sight,

"Merry Christmas to All, and to All a Good Night."